The Ghosts of 2012

by

Graham Hurley

DORSET COUNTY COUNCIL	
205012562 N	
PETERS	£5.99
26-Aug-2009	

First published in 2009 in Great Britain by
Barrington Stoke Ltd
18 Walker Street, Edinburgh, EH3 7LP

www.barringtonstoke.co.uk

ISBN: 978-1-84299-663-8

Printed in Great Britain by Bell & Bain Ltd

A Note from the Author

This is a story about sport and politics – the two things I love. I've been sports-mad since school. I played in all the teams and ran too. I made decent times in the 100 and 200 metre sprints. As I got older, I also got interested in politics – how we elect people to organise our lives and what happens then.

We've started to take our freedoms for granted. Fewer and fewer people bother to vote, even in General Elections. No one seems to care who's making the laws. At the same time, governments have become keener and keener to make an impact. They want the rest of the world to notice what they do.

Sports-wise, the Olympic Games is the biggest stage of all ... and in 2012, the Games will be coming to London. But what about the credit-crunch we're facing now? And what about the huge problems that lie beyond?

Put those two events together and this story is what you get. So welcome to *The Ghosts of 2012*.

To Freya and Milo,
with love

With special thanks to our readers:
Kate King
Jamie R.
Mary Mullan
Suzanne Louden

Contents

Chapter 1
Winning

Sometimes in life you get moments that stick out ... you remember them for ever. And this was definitely one of them.

It was July 2010. The UK Athletics team had been at the European Championships all week, and we were at the airport in Spain waiting for an early flight home. The team had done well and some of us had done even better than that. In the 3000 metres steeplechase, I'd won with a Personal Best of 7.54.02 minutes, just half a second outside the World Record.

The steeplechase is a really tough race – 28 hurdles and seven water jumps – and no one in Europe had ever run the course as fast as me. We were two years away from the London 2012 Olympics and I knew I had a real chance of winning the gold.

At the airport, they'd put all the athletes in the VIP lounge. The flight was due to leave at 06.10. I'd phoned Anna straight after yesterday's race and told her what had happened but she'd seen it already on TV. Anna hates getting up early but no way would she not be at Heathrow to give me a hug when I got back. That, at least, was the plan.

Six o'clock came and went. There was no sign of our flight. Then a Spanish official came in and had a brief chat with our team manager. As soon as he'd gone, the manager shut the door and told us to gather round.

"Guys ..." he said, "it seems there's been some kind of take-over back home. I can't give you details but UK air space has been closed.

No flights in. No flights out. Until things are clearer, I'm afraid we're stuck here."

We waited at the airport to see what would happen next. There were two big TV screens in the VIP lounge and both of them were showing news reports. The top story was what was happening in the UK. Just after ten o'clock a shot of Downing Street came up on the screen. Armed soldiers were standing outside the door of Number Ten and the reporter announced that we'd be going live to talk to someone inside.

That someone was a Field Marshal. A top army chief. He was sitting at a desk with a photo of the King behind him. He talked for about five minutes. He said that the country was in crisis and that the Interim Military Council had taken over. He said that there was no reason for anyone to panic and that things would just carry on as normal. As soon as possible, the new government would be back in office, but for the time being the UK would be under the control of the military authorities.

An hour or so later, the Spanish told us that our flight was ready for boarding. UK air space was open again and we'd be back at Heathrow by lunchtime. That was good news but most of us were still staring at the TV screens. How come a bunch of generals could suddenly take power like that? In the UK, of all places? And what on earth would happen next?

All this, of course, is now history ... one of those moments that no one British will ever forget.

****

Anna wasn't at the airport when we got back. That was a big let down. I said good-bye to the rest of the team and took the train to Bristol. Everything looked pretty normal. You wouldn't have known there'd been a big army take-over.

Home is a top-floor flat near the docks. I let myself in and dumped my bag. Anna was hunched over the phone, talking to her friend Kelly. Kelly is seriously bad news. I waited until Anna was off the phone. A hug for winning might have been nice. Instead, she nodded up at the telly. More shots of Downing Street.

"You know what they've done now?" she asked me.

She told me everything that had happened. Parliament shut. Strict media control. Even rumours of mass arrests of people thought to be a danger to the new military government. To be honest, much of this stuff passed me by. It sounded like the script of a movie that would never get made. I said so. That was a mistake.

"You don't believe me?" Anna snapped. "You don't think it's important? Centuries of freedom, of civil rights? Gone ..." she clicked her fingers "... just like that?"

Anna's always been very political. And done things about it too. It's one of the reasons I fell in love with her. Show her a good cause and she'll organise a protest in seconds. She was still staring at me, still waiting for an answer.

I did my best to explain.

"I'm an athlete," I said. "I just get on with what I'm good at, what I'm best at. And just now it's really working for me."

Anna couldn't believe what I'd said. "So it's fine by you, then? A load of fascist generals taking over?" she asked.

"I didn't say that. It's just all ..." I wanted to find the right word. "A bit sudden."

"But that's the way it happens, Joe. That's the way they plan it. And you know the saddest thing of all? No one cares a stuff."

I thought about this for a moment. Even I knew that things hadn't been brilliant in the UK over the last few months. The housing crash, the unemployment, petrol at £2 a litre, food and power prices that just went up and up, the collapse of yet another bank – the news never got any better. My dad had said he'd never expected to see soup kitchens back in British cities or tents for homeless families on parks and recreation grounds. Turned out he'd been wrong.

"Maybe it's for the best," I said softly. "Maybe we need a bit of a sort-out."

To my surprise, Anna agreed. The government that these new army guys had chucked out had been pathetic and hopeless.

"You heard about the thing in Afghanistan last week?" she asked.

I nodded. The Taliban had flown a plane full of explosives into the main British camp. More than 200 of our blokes had been killed. Maybe that was why the Generals had taken control.

"So what can we do about it?" I asked.

"I dunno. Something. Anything. Kelly's got some ideas." She shrugged. "I dunno."

We stared at each other, lost for words. Then I said, why didn't we have a drink to celebrate my medal in Spain? Last time I'd looked, there were cans of Stella in the fridge.

Anna shook her head. I've seen that look at countless athletics meets. Total commitment. Total focus.

"I'm outta here, Joe. There's no way we're not going to fight it," she said.

She was gone in minutes. And I didn't know when I'd see her again.

Chapter 2
Losing

I missed her. Badly. The last time she'd gone off, she hadn't come back for a couple of months. That time she'd left after we'd had a monster argument. I'd been so angry that I hadn't tried and get in touch. This time was different. We'd been living together since Christmas. We were good for each other, made each other laugh. She'd always put up with me – with the crazy dedication I had to put in to make it big-time in athletics. We fitted perfectly around each other's lives. I didn't expect her to just vanish like that.

I waited a day, then tried to phone her. A computerised voice told me that the number I'd rung was no longer valid. Had she really left me? Or had she put herself out of contact on purpose? All I could do was wait for her to get in touch. Nothing happened.

By the end of the week there was still no word. I was desperate. I knew where Kelly lived, and after the day's training was over I drove to her house. I knocked a few times and at last a bloke came to the door. I'd seen him with Kelly at some music gigs. I told him about Anna.

"She was here a few days ago, mate. Stayed over. Then Kelly told me they were both going underground. Haven't seen them since."

"Really?" I was trying to take the news in.

"Yeah. No shit."

I stared at him as he stepped back into the house. Underground?

****

The autumn came. My training was going from bad to worse. I was failing to hit the times I needed and some days I could only just get myself out of bed. My coach told me I had a glucose deficiency and gave me special supplements to take, but he was wrong. I was lonely. Anna had been the biggest part of my life. We'd grown up together deep in the countryside in East Devon. Her brother, Rob Capper, was still my best mate. Now she'd gone I was desperate to find something – *anything* – to ease the pain. The only thing I knew, the only thing I could trust, was my sport.

Top athletes live in a bubble. All you care about is running faster than anyone else on the planet over a set distance. You target one race – eight minutes of your life – to take on the best guys in the world and beat them. For me, that race had to be the 3000 metres steeplechase at the 2012 Olympics.

The stadium, in London, was already taking shape. I had photos of it pasted up all over the flat. It was the first thing I saw when I woke up in the morning. I had another shot in the bathroom, I saw it every time I used the mirror to shave. I even had a photo on the back of the loo door. The running track itself was not yet laid but I could half close my eyes, imagine the nine lanes curving away at the end of the straight, hear the roar of the crowd as I fought through the field and headed for the line. That image kept me going. It was a winter of the hardest training I'd ever done. In a couple of years' time, that steeplechase gold had to be mine. Nothing was more important. Not even Anna.

Then I met Carmen. She was new on the UK team. She trained, like me, in Bristol but lived in Bath. Carmen ran the 200 metres and had posted some brilliant times. She was half-English, half-Caribbean, and the media loved her because of her looks. She was tall and slim, and her skin tone – a silky dark olive – had twice put her on the covers of up-market men's magazines. I began to train at times when I knew we'd bump into each other on the track. Then came the evening when I asked her out for a drink. We talked lap times, split times, sponsorship deals with the big sports companies, locker room gossip about who was shagging who. Pretty soon, we were living together.

We were both serious about our sport. Our lives were a perfect fit. We had another passion too – motorbikes. Every week-end we'd bomb out of Bristol and ride the country roads up across Exmoor. I'd even bought Carmen a set of sleek black leathers which she wore like a second skin.

By now, on the track, I was back in the medal zone. I went to loads of meets and won every race. Carmen was running fantastic times, as well, and in the eyes of the media we'd become the Golden Couple.

My sponsor loved this kind of coverage. He'd taken the train from London to invite us both out for a meal. He had a big surprise for us. He laid the brochure on the table the moment we walked into the restaurant. On the front was a picture of a big glossy sports car. Carmen and I had never dreamed of owning a Porsche Carrera. This one could be ours. What was the catch?

The sponsor was an American called Nicko. Americans tend to be blunt.

"Listen, guys." He was looking at me. "The deal's simple. You get the loan of the Porsche in return for selling that bike of yours. The last thing we need right now is an accident. OK?"

Anyone half-sane wouldn't have given this a moment's thought but Carmen loved my old Kawasaki – the Kwacker – as much as I did. We both looked at each other and asked for some time to think about it. Big mistake.

Next day was Saturday. For once, I'd taken a day off training. We talked for ages and at last decided to say yes to the Porsche but treat ourselves to one last mind-blowing ride on the Kwacker.

****

We headed for Exmoor. The beauty of the moor is the lack of trees and hedges. The roads up there wind and dip and you can see for miles. At top speed, the Kwacker can hit 145 mph.

Towards the end of the afternoon, I badly missed a corner. There was loose gravel, too, but it was my fault. The ambulance got us both to hospital within the hour. I wasn't too knocked about but Carmen was unconscious for two days. At the end of the week, the doctor took me aside and told me that she had multiple fractures in both legs. Her left ankle was a mess and her left knee would have to be

totally rebuilt. She'd be lucky to walk again,
let alone run.

Chapter 3
Anna Again

For reasons I don't understand, Nicko still went ahead and we got the Porsche. Maybe, under all that Manhattan aggression, he was a nicer bloke than I'd thought. Or maybe he'd already ordered the Porsche. In any case, I rapidly became an expert at folding Carmen into the passenger seat of this beautiful car. She was aware of how people looked at her or stared at us when we were in traffic. She said the pain was good for her. Brave girl.

Slowly, as time went by, she began to walk again. She saw a physio for four sessions a week and worked hard at getting back up on her feet. But by the time summer came round I think we both knew that her running days were over.

She spent hours on the internet looking up doctors and operations for legs that had been as badly broken as hers. She got hold of the contact details for a doctor in Arizona in the US. She talked to him on the phone a couple of times, and sent him a thick envelope of her X-rays. This guy was an expert in sports injuries and after he'd taken a look he told her that the real problem was the knee. He'd developed a new hi-tech operation and he promised her a 70 per cent chance of full mobility once he'd done the op for her. The only problem was the price tag. $65,000. Plus expenses.

By now, the Interim Military Council had been running the country for a full year. They'd created jobs and they'd also helped local councils to buy up thousands of the homes that no one could afford any more.

They rented them out really cheaply. People felt better about life. Once again, they had money in their pockets and roofs over their heads. There was still no Parliament but no one missed the politicians. Other countries had begun to invest money in the UK now and the pound was strong again. At last, we counted for something in the world.

The best news for us was a big pat on the back for UK Sport. We'd done well at the Beijing Olympics in 2008 and in 2010 the England team had made the final in the World Cup. The generals saw that sport was really important and would help to put the Great back into Britain. With the 2012 Games about to happen in London, and the Olympic Village taking shape by the day, the Generals decided to double the money they were giving the Olympic squad. I was already getting lots of support from media and sponsorship fees. With the extra money from the Generals I now stood a fighting chance of flying Carmen to Arizona.

And not before time. Slowly, day by day, she was becoming a different person. The sunshine had left her. The light had died in her eyes. She just lay around the flat, doing nothing, and began to put on weight. It wasn't that I minded doing the cooking, or anything else for that matter. It was just the feeling of living with someone who was fast becoming a stranger.

Then Anna turned up.

She came to the flat on a Sunday evening in early November. Carmen was asleep in the bedroom. It was pouring with rain and Anna was soaked. One look at her grin and I knew exactly why I'd fallen in love with her.

I got her a towel. When she stepped out of the bathroom, she was wearing Carmen's dressing gown. There was lots of Carmen's medical stuff in the bathroom and she asked why. The question threw me a bit. Our accident had been all over the press and TV but Anna wasn't tuned in. She didn't know anything about it. When I told her about what had happened she said she was really sorry. Bad shit.

I asked Anna what she'd been up to but she wouldn't tell me.

"Doesn't matter," she said. "Just stuff."

"Is Kelly still involved?" I asked.

"Yeah," Anna nodded.

"But you won't tell me any more?" I went on.

"I can't. I just wanted to catch up, see how you were."

"I'm fine." I shrugged. "My training's going OK. I run silly distances every day, just like always. Everyone seems to think I'm a cert for the Games. They might even ask me to carry the flag at the opening ceremony."

21

"And you'd say yes?" Anna looked shocked.

"I might," I said.

"You've heard about the internment camps? The exiles? All that?" Anna didn't seem to understand me.

I nodded. There were plenty of rumours if you could be bothered to take an interest. How most of the country's thinkers, writers and teachers had fled to mainland Europe. How the rest had been banged up in special camps.

"And you're really happy with all this stuff?" Anna was frowning now.

"Of course I'm not. But life goes on."

"Sure. And yours couldn't be sweeter," Anna turned away.

That was a cheap shot. Training isn't pain-free, not the way we have to do it. And nor is living with someone you've turned into a cripple. I began to protest but Anna beat me to it.

"Listen ..." She put her hand on mine. "I'm sorry. I shouldn't have said that. It's just the whole thing, the Generals, what they're up to, what they've done to us. And it's not just the Generals any more, Joe, it's the guys behind them, the people from the City. This has become a country run by banks and by businessmen. They control everything, even you. The Generals are a front. In a way they're as helpless as we are."

I was trying to work out how Anna knew so much about what was going on. The Generals controlled the newspapers. Same with TV. And radio. All we heard was what they wanted us to hear.

"I use the internet." She gave me a couple of websites, both in France. "Be careful what PC you use if you log on. They're scanning everything these days."

She got up. Carmen's dressing gown fell open. Anna was naked underneath. She grinned down at me, then went back into the bathroom. Back in the sitting room, moments later, she'd pulled her jeans on, still soaking wet.

"I like your stadium shots," she said. "I'm here to wish you luck. You deserve it, you lovely man."

She looked at me for a long moment, then bent to give me a kiss. I reached up for her, wanting more, but she shook her head. Seconds later, she was out of the door. Only later did I work out what was really happening. She'd come to say goodbye.

****

Back to that winter. Things were tough. Carmen had shut herself away and was more and more distant. I made up for that by training even harder.

Our last pre-Olympics Christmas came and went. I was keen to spend it with my folks back in Devon but Carmen never went out any more. She hated leaving the flat and the thought of the trip home to Bath for a few days with her mum and dad filled her with horror. And so we spent a quiet time looking at shit television and waiting for the duck to roast. It was the only Christmas Day I've ever been glad to go for a run.

The New Year was the same story. To be frank, I only stayed sane because I was training so hard. By Easter, I knew in my heart that I could take the world record. My coach knew it too, and so did Nicko, my sponsor. He'd started talking about another new car, something even flasher. If he really wanted to win my heart, I said he should take Carmen to Phoenix and buy her a new life. He smiled his Nicko smile and said he'd think about it.

****

Early summer 2012 was tense. The UK Olympic trials were due to take place in June. Even my coach, an old East German who'd pretty much seen everything in athletics, was pretty confident we had nothing to worry about. The trials were held in a stadium in the West Midlands. I knew every one of the athletes on the start line and I knew for certain I could leave them all for dead. This feeling of total confidence, the feeling that I *owned* the race, was what you needed at my level. It turned out I was right, too. I won by nearly 30 metres. A place in the 2012 Olympic team was mine.

Chapter 4
Ghosts

Next morning, back home, I got a text from my best mate, Rob Capper, Anna's brother. She'd vanished. I remember staring at that text for minutes on end. I could see Anna, that last time she'd been in the flat. I could hear her voice. *You lovely man*, she'd said.

I knew perfectly well that nothing, *nothing*, should break my focus at this point in my running career. I was six weeks off the Olympic Games. Years and years of the hardest work I'd ever done had put me within touching distance of a medal, something only a very few athletes would ever experience. And yet. And yet ...

I phoned Rob and asked what exactly had happened. When he said he couldn't talk on the mobile I knew it was serious. From Bristol, the Porsche could make Devon in just over an hour. Despite the motorway cameras, I did it in less.

Rob left school at 18 and joined the Royal Marines. After a spell in Afghanistan, he was now an instructor at the Commando Training Centre, which happened to be in East Devon where we'd both lived. Just up the road was a pub called The Puffing Billy.

Rob and I met in the back bar. It turned out that he'd been keeping a close eye on Anna for the past year or so. He was her brother, after all. He knew the risks she was taking and had done his best to keep her out of real trouble. Until a few days ago.

"She's been lifted," he said.

"*Lifted?*" I asked. "What does that mean?"

"Arrested. Scooped up. Ghosted. Call it what you like. The people in charge have no sense of humour, mate. Cross the line and you vanish."

"But what has she done?" I wanted to know.

Rob wasn't sure. He knew about the foreign websites. He knew how Anna and her friends wanted to know more about the Generals and challenge what was going on. But that was all he knew. What Anna was really doing was just guess-work.

"It could be anything," he said. "At worst I suppose she could be involved in the bombings, though I don't think so. She'd be clueless around explosives."

I nodded. There'd been a series of small bomb explosions in the Midlands and the North. No one in the media had reported them but word had spread. With the Olympic Games so close, this was the last thing the Generals needed.

"So where has Anna been living?" I asked him.

"Lots of addresses but mostly in Exeter. Kelly phoned me last night. She said they lifted her on Wednesday afternoon in broad daylight on Cathedral Close. Kelly was giving me all kinds of grief about it, but, you know what? I think that bitch shopped her."

Like me, Rob had never been keen on Kelly. Now he was sure she was working for the Generals, spying for them. These days, you trusted no one.

"So where's Anna?" I asked again.

Rob thought they'd taken her to the local internment centre. In the hard times, loads of shops had gone bust. Big superstores and businesses on trading estates lay empty and the Generals had turned some of them into prisons for people they didn't like.

"My guess is they've banged her up in the old KidzStuff shed beside the motorway," Rob said.

"Is there any way we can check that?" I asked.

"Yeah. We're on stand-by at the Commando Centre in case anything kicks off. It's our job to keep an eye on things at the internment camp. We get updated prisoner lists every morning. I can ask to do a security check on the place. Piece of piss."

"So how many prisoners – I mean, 'internees' – are we talking about?" I said.

"With my kid sister? 864," Rob replied.

****

I took this news back with me to Bristol. Rob wasn't sure about what the Generals actually *did* with people like Anna but I sensed a darkness that went well beyond the one-time KidzStuff superstore. When I got back to the flat, Carmen was out. So far, I'd never logged on to the foreign websites Anna had left me. I found the note she scribbled. I started with www.maquis.fr.com.

The site was amazing. There was a list of recent bomb incidents plus a long list of people who'd vanished. I scrolled down the list. It was like reading the names off a war memorial. What had happened to these people? Where were they?

In another part of the same website were Resistance blogs from different parts of the UK. Just writing and posting this stuff must have been risky and I felt the first prickles of shame that I'd never thought hard enough about the Generals – our new government. I read the stories now. They were mind-blowing. Stories about people banged up for making jokes about the Generals. Stories about kids – *kids* – who'd been tortured into betraying their parents.

I stared at the screen. This was a big moment for me. I felt as helpless as everyone else in the country when it came to taking on the Generals – they were simply too powerful – but what I *did* have was celebrity. People knew my name. And from the Generals' point of view, I mattered. Especially with London 2012 coming up in six weeks.

There was a corner of the website where you could add comments of your own. After a while I began to write. I said who I was and I said that I was really worried about what was going on. As an athlete, I was really glad to be running for my country but I was no longer sure that I really belonged here. Not under this government. Not with things the way they were. And, if that was the case, how could I possibly compete?

I read what I'd written. I wasn't at all sure where it would lead, or even what good it might do, but I knew people would see it. I was still reading my comments when Carmen came back. I didn't hear her let herself in. The first

I knew was her standing behind me, reading what I'd just written.

"You're crazy," she said softly.

"You think so?" I looked up at her, then hit the Send button.

Chapter 5
Pressure

The first person to get in touch was my coach. He rang the next morning, half past seven. I was to get my arse over to the training complex by nine o'clock. He wanted to talk to me.

I left Carmen asleep. She was worn out after our argument last night and I was in no mood to wake her up. I hoofed the Porsche across the city and was stepping into my coach's office spot on nine o'clock.

I've been with Erik Boehm for nearly four years. He's old and grouchy but what he knows about athletics – and athletes – is awesome. In East Germany, long ago, before the Berlin Wall came down, he was a world-class 800 metres runner. Everyone gives him major respect.

For once, he didn't offer me one of his special luke-warm coffees. When I tried to read the latest e-mail on his PC, he turned the screen away.

First he checked that the posting on the Maquis website really had been me. I said it was. He looked at me hard for a moment and I didn't have a clue what he was thinking. Then he nodded at the door. Beyond the door was a bank of running machines.

"No one ever said this would be easy, Joe," Erik said softly.

"It's not the training," I told him. "I can deal with that."

"I know, I know. But these people, the Generals, have got inside your head, haven't they? And you know what? You have to chase them out again. There's no room, Joe. They mustn't distract you. There's no room for distractions like them."

"Is that what they are?" I was thinking of Anna banged up in some internment camp. *"Distractions?"*

"Of course. For you. For me. For everyone. Get on with life. It's there for you. And so is a medal." Erik leaned forward. "One day these people will go. Trust me. One day you will wake up and they'll be gone."

"Just like that?" I didn't believe him.

"Sure. And you know what? Every day they stay in your head is for them another little victory. You don't want that, Joe. You don't want them to win."

"But they have won," I pointed out. "And that's the problem."

****

When I left the office I promised I'd think things over. We both knew that meant nothing. I did an hour or so of weights, then some splits and repetitions on the track, and then cut the rest of my training and drove home. I knew I needed a real conversation with Carmen but when I got back to the flat she was out. I thought about waiting for her but in the end I left her a note. *Out running*, I told her. *Normal circuit.*

Normal circuit meant a special corner of the Mendip Hills I'd pretty much made my own. Forty minutes in the Porsche, and I was heading up the first steep climb, knowing I'd be glad of the shade of the big trees at the top of the hill. I ran a seven-mile loop, testing myself against the clock, forcing the pace when every muscle in my body was begging for rest. That way, as ever, I could bury the uglier thoughts. By the time I'd finished the circuit, the endorphins had kicked in and I was cruising.

As I came round the spur of the last hill, I stopped. I'd left the Porsche in the same lay-by as always. Behind it was a black Mercedes saloon. As I was watching, a bulky figure I knew got out. He saw me and waved. Nicko. My sponsor. He must have rung and talked to Carmen, I thought. And she must have read my note and told him where I was.

The back of the Mercedes was empty. Nicko asked me to climb in. There was a blonde woman in the car – older than me and in a beautiful silk suit. Every time we meet, it's Nicko who does the talking. This afternoon was just the same. He told me he was really happy with my Olympic trials performance. I'd blown the rest of the guys away. Brilliant running, buddy.

He was sitting in the front of the car, his body twisted round to talk to me. Now came the real conversation.

"So put me right, Joe. Tell me all this shit I'm reading on the internet isn't true. Tell me some guy out there's stolen your name. Danny's been working on a press release. You wanna hear it? Danny, go ahead ..."

Danny was the blonde woman. She was French, and was in charge of the company's European publicity operation. She began to read from the press release. Sexy accent.

"*Olympic gold medal contender Joe Purnell today denied any connection with the blog posted 48 hours ago on a number of foreign websites. Purnell, whose recent races have earned him top world ranking for the 3000 metres steeplechase, was angry about the theft of his identity. He promised legal action against the owners of the website if anything similar should be posted again. 'Like any Olympic athlete, I'm running for my country,' said Purnell, 'and I'm proud of it.'*"

Nicko gave me the big corporate grin. The conversation was nearly over.

"Short and sweet, Joe," he said. "We need to knock this thing on the head. Anything you want to add, you just go right ahead. Danny, you gotta pen?"

Danny produced a fountain pen and passed the press release back to me. I didn't take the pen.

"You gotta problem with any of this stuff, Joe?" Nicko asked.

"Yeah." I was looking out at the hills. "I'm afraid I have."

****

I was home by six. I let myself into the flat, called Carmen's name, got no answer. I thought she must still be out. I stepped into the bathroom and stripped to take a shower. Then I realised that the door to the cupboard where she keeps all her pills was open. I called her name again, then went through to our bedroom. The curtains were pulled against the sunshine but in the gloom I could see the shape of Carmen's body on top of the duvet. Her back was turned to me and one arm was stretched towards the bedside table. On the table I saw the plastic bottle of painkillers she often used. It was empty.

I stepped across to her, bent low, gave her a gentle shake. She shifted a little and muttered something I didn't catch. She was cold to the touch and her breathing was very light. I was about to fetch my mobile from the bathroom when I caught sight of the note folded beside the empty bottle of tablets. When she's upset or angry, Carmen writes in capitals.

YOUR FAULT, the note read. BASTARD.

Chapter 6
Combat Damage

I stayed with Carmen in the back of the ambulance. They wheeled her, still unconscious, into A&E and told me to find a seat in the waiting area. I sat there for the best part of four hours. I felt numb. *Your fault, bastard*, I kept thinking.

Around half past nine, three young guys came in. One of them was limping and had a nasty cut on his head. They were looking for trouble. One of them gave a waste-paper bin a kick. Then his mate looked at me and did a double take. He'd seen me on the telly. He wanted to shake my hand, make a real night of it, tell the world what a hero I was. I was trying to calm him down when two Bubs arrived. The nurse behind the desk must have pressed the panic button.

Bubs were what we called the new breed of private security guys that were everywhere. Bubs stands for 'Big Ugly Bastards'. They rode around in big 4x4 pick-up trucks, black paintwork, black windows. They wore baggy camouflage suits, thick-soled high-laced boots and combat helmets. They carried big American assault guns. They took no shit from anyone and it was impossible to get their name or ID. They wore wraparound shades and they all looked the same.

Now, the Bubs drew batons and bundled the youths across the waiting area and through a pair of swing doors marked 'Fire Exit'. The coffee machine was beside the doors. I went over, found some small change, and peered through the glass panel on one of the doors.

The doors led to the stairs. I could see the two Bubs giving the youths a battering. All three youths were on the floor, trying to cover their heads. I pushed through the doors and tried to pull the Bubs off. One of them, the smaller of the two, spun round and cracked me across the side of my face with his baton. Seconds later, still staggering, I became aware of the hot, coppery taste of my own blood. The Bub nodded towards the swing doors.

"I'd get that seen to, son." He touched his own face. "Looks nasty."

A nurse in A&E stitched the wound and gave me a couple of paracetamols. No one seemed interested in my story about the Bubs. "These days," the nurse said with a shrug, "that kind of stuff happens all the time." A couple of minutes after I'd returned to the waiting area, my mobile began to ring. By now, I'd had word that Carmen was pulling through.

It was my agent Paul March on the phone. Like Nicko and Erik Boehm, he must have got the word about my little outburst on the website.

"Listen," he said. "I'm in Bristol. We need to talk."

I explained about Carmen, but already the phone had gone dead. Branzino's, he'd said. As soon as you like.

****

Branzino's was Paul's favourite Bristol restaurant. We always meet there when he comes down. At first he looked at me as if he didn't know who I was. Then he saw it was me.

"What happened?" He was staring at the line of stitches above my right eye.

I explained about the Bubs and the fight at A&E but he wasn't really listening. He was more interested in my posting on the French website.

"You've upset people," he said.

"I bet."

"Important people. Powerful people. You're lucky this once. They know that you don't mean it."

"Who told them that?" I asked.

"Me."

"Then you'd be wrong." I was still thinking about the Bubs beating the crap out of three harmless young pissheads.

"Listen, Joe. I'm here to look after your best interests. In this case, I'm trying to protect you from career suicide," Paul said.

"Suicide's a tricky word just now, Paul," I muttered.

"Yeah? Listen, I'm sorry about Carmen but I mean it. Pull out of the Games and you'll never run again."

"Who says?" I asked him.

"They do. You want to know how? At best you'll get a lifetime ban. Next best, they'll break your legs. Worst case? Let's not go there."

That sounded like a threat. Paul broke off to OK a bottle of red. Then he was back in my face again.

"You won't remember the '36 Olympics, Joe, but there was a black guy running, an American sprinter, Jesse Owens. The Nazis had set the Games up as this big advert for what they were doing, what they were about. Their team was full of huge strapping blond white guys who were going to steamroller everyone. Except they didn't. Because Jesse Owens dicked them all. By winning. You could do the same thing."

"To the Generals?" I wanted to know.

"Yeah."

"By taking the gold?" I went on.

"Sure. And that matters, doesn't it?"

By now, I had a headache. The inside of my skull felt like it was going to burst. I was way past making any kind of decision on anything. Instead I was looking at the bottle of wine. Paul reached for my glass. I shook my head.

"Any chance of something stronger?" I said.

"No problem, Joe." He summoned the waiter. "First sane thing you've said all night."

Chapter 7
Limbo Land

They came for me at half past three in the morning. To be honest, I don't remember how I got back from the restaurant. All I can remember is a blazing row with my agent. The fact that I'd drunk half a bottle of grappa didn't help. When Paul asked me to promise that I'd behave myself and not annoy the Generals again, I told him to fuck off. I was the fastest steeplechaser on the planet. I'd do it my way.

I woke up to a splintering noise as they smashed open the front door of my flat. Then I was looking at three armed Bubs standing over my bed – helmets, visors, body armour, the lot. They pulled me out of bed and told me to get dressed. I tried to make it down the stairs towards the street but fell over twice. The second time they gave me a kick.

The back of the 4x4 stank of vomit and bleach. I sat between two of the Bubs. In a weird way, I felt too dazed to be frightened. This whole thing was like a dream – surreal.

The guy behind the wheel drove like a maniac. In no time at all we were out of the city and pulling a hard left into one of the trading estates beside the M5 motorway. I saw the Halfords Superstore and the Ikea sign in the distance before we slowed for some kind of check-point. A hard white light shone down on sandbags and rolls of razor wire. The barrier went up and we stopped outside a Portakabin.

I was pushed inside and told to strip. Photos were taken, my personal details noted and everything in my pockets tucked away in an envelope. Only when I showed my ID card did the woman behind the desk believe that I was me.

"I saw you on telly," she grunted. "So how come you ended up here?"

Good question. There was a shower next to the Portakabin. An old guy in an orange jumpsuit with a logo on the back hosed me down. When I asked why, he just laughed. Welcome to the world of DIY.

They gave me an orange jumpsuit of my own and I was marched across the car park to the superstore. More razor wire. More sandbags. Inside, the racks and shelves were still full of the things you needed for DIY – nails, paint tins, light bulbs – but the floors were packed with sleeping orange bodies. The lights were low and it was hard to be certain but there must have been hundreds of internees in there. There were guards with automatic rifles everywhere. Totally surreal.

They found me an oblong of concrete in Wall Fixings. I was tossed a thin bed roll and a blanket. The guy next to me grunted, turned over, then went back to sleep again. The blanket was crusted with something evil and the whole place stank. I knew I was never going to get any sleep. For the first time in years, I was no longer in control of my own life.

Next morning, we all lined up for a cup of stewed tea. The guy I'd slept beside shuffled up to me in the queue. He turned out to be a black stand-up comic from the West Midlands. His name was Marcus. He'd done a couple of gigs in a club in Plymouth and some of his more edgy jokes had gone down badly with the Generals. He wasn't sure – it was easy to lose track – but he thought he'd spent at least a few months in the warehouse. He was always asking to talk to someone in charge but they ignored him. When I asked him what would happen next he just shrugged.

"It's limbo-land, man," he said. "Ain't no clocks. Ain't no daylight. Ain't no nothing."

The thought of spending serious time in Wall Fixings was hard to grasp, but I was luckier than Marcus. The guards came for me hours later. I think it was around midday. In an office at the front of the building I was allowed to have a plate of biscuits and a cup of proper coffee. Sitting beside a middle-aged man in army uniform was someone I knew. My coach. Erik Boehm.

The officer told me that Carmen was out of hospital and had been shipped back to her parents' place in Bath. When I asked whether she'd left me any kind of message he scribbled himself a note and said he'd look into it. In the meantime, I was to listen to my coach.

Erik looked really uneasy.

"I've been talking to some people," he said, "and they're ready to offer you a deal."

"What kind of deal?" I asked.

"They'll let you out of here," he said, "but in return you must promise to run your race. You must also watch what you say in all the media interviews. You turn up for the 3000 metres steeplechase. And then you win."

"And if I say no?" I wanted to know.

"Then things will be a bit different."

"Like how?"

Erik shrugged. He couldn't say because he didn't know. At this point, the officer leant forward over the desk.

"Maybe this is simpler than you think it is." He was looking at me. "No one in this country is bigger than the Generals. And that, my friend, includes you."

My fingers moved up to touch the stitches above my eye. I believed him.

Erik asked me how I felt. I said fine. I was still looking at the officer. My mind was racing.

"You're holding a woman called Anna Capper," I said. "The moment you let her go, I'll do whatever you want."

The officer looked back at me and made a note of the name. Erik slumped in his chair. The meeting was over.

****

I returned to my blanket and my bed roll. By now, the news seemed to have spread that an Olympic gold medal prospect was banged up in Wall Fixings. I spent most of the night fending off different sports fans. Then, towards what felt like dawn, came a very different conversation.

When the guards weren't looking, I'd rolled under the storage racks and found myself in Painting Accessories. Deep down I knew they were going to let me out, and before that happened I wanted to see as much of the internment centre as I could. As I crawled out from under the rack, I felt that the cut above my eye was bleeding again. The guy nearest to me had seen it too. He had some loo roll stashed away. He started to clean me up.

Before long he'd put a name to my face. It turned out that he was a serious fell runner. He lived in a tiny village in Somerset and over the past few years he'd got to know every corner of the hills around his house. We talked about distance running for a while, what we each took from it, then he told me about his neighbour.

"The guy's some kind of freelance journalist. He drinks a bit, too, and the last time he had a skinful in the pub he told me this story he'd picked up from a friend of his in Ireland. Something about dead bodies on a beach."

"What happened?" I asked.

"He wouldn't say but next morning he came to see me, really hung over, and swore me to silence. Said I wasn't to tell anyone a word about the Irish thing."

"How come?" I wanted to know more.

"He's scared shitless about our new leaders. He says he's on their books already and no way does he want to end up in a place like this."

I trusted the guy in Painting Accessories. He said that if I got out, I was welcome to borrow his place in Somerset. The hills, he said, were great for running. He scribbled down a handful of local routes and told me how to find the village and the spare key to his cottage. He also gave me the name of the journalist. Before I got the call to the next interview, I made sure I could remember the lot.

They let me out the next morning, after a brief interview. In return for the promise of Anna's release, I agreed to keep my mouth shut and run the 3000 metres steeplechase. Looking back, I don't think either side was ever going to deliver on the deal, but by that time I'd had more than enough of Wall Fixings. Anna was right. Living under this lot was like a surrender of all you believed in. By mid-afternoon, with a bagful of spare clothes, I was heading down the M5 towards Devon.

Chapter 8

Somerset

Rob was home from the Commando Centre by the time I arrived. He lived with his partner and their two kids in a rented house at the back of a seaside town called Exmouth. He'd read the blog I'd posted on the French website. When he saw the state of my face he thought the Generals had sent someone to beat me up because of the blog. In a way, it was true. Nowadays, the Bubs could do whatever they liked. It certainly didn't pay to cross these guys.

When I told him about Wall Fixings and the deal that had got me out, he shook his head. The Regime were promising to let Anna out once the Games were over. Like me, he didn't believe it.

"So what are you going to do?" he asked.

I told him about Carmen. I'd phoned her at her parents' place in Bath but we were shouting at each other within seconds. She said I was stubborn and selfish. In her view, I'd blown my chance for Olympic gold and as an ex-athlete herself, she found that beyond belief. She also knew that I'd blown any prospect of funding her American operation. Nicko had rung her and more or less told her so. Maybe that was why she'd taken the tablets. Nice.

"So what next?" Rob asked again.

I told him I was going to try and find Anna. He thought I was mad. I'd seen the inside of an internment camp. I must know by now just how tightly the Generals had got the country stitched up. Anna was just one name and there were tens of thousands who'd vanished. Where would I start?

"I'm not sure," I said. "But the point is that people know me. They've seen me on telly. They've read about me in the papers. I'm a bit of a celeb and if I can use that to help Anna then ..." I shrugged "... I will. No way am I going to be running for these bastards."

Big moment. I stared at Rob. I'd never felt so sure of anything in my life. No way was I going to let myself down.

"But how do you get at them?" he asked.

I told him about the things I'd just heard from the internee I'd chatted to last night.

"The guy's got a neighbour who's some kind of journalist. He's dug up a story in Ireland, something that might embarrass the Generals. The guy's an hour away. I'm going to talk to him. If I can use my celeb status to tell the story, something might give. We've got a chance to show up the Generals."

"When are you planning to meet him?" Rob was looking at his watch.

"Now."

****

Rob insisted on coming with me. The village in Somerset was tiny, tucked into a fold of the Quantock Hills. There was a storm brewing out towards the west and I could smell rain in the air. One of the three cottages at the end of the village had to belong to the journalist.

We got lucky with our first knock. He was a tall guy with thinning hair. When he saw us at his door the colour drained from his face.

We invited ourselves in. The last 48 hours had totally changed how I felt about pretty much everything. Like Rob, I knew that the Generals would be watching my every move.

The whole country was covered by CCTV. I knew I didn't have much time before the Generals worked out what I was doing.

The cottage was dark, with stone floors and damp patches on the walls. When the journo asked what we wanted, Rob told him that we'd been sent to collect his notes on the Irish story. We'd agreed on the way to Somerset we'd tell him that. It would be a neat way of finding out if the Irish story even existed.

It did. But the journo had recognised me and wanted to know what the hell we were doing.

Rob showed him his Royal Marines ID. The journo looked at it for a moment, then said he'd have to make a phone call to a contact in the Regime. Just to check. Rob and I looked at each other. We both knew that call would blow our cover. And set the Generals onto us.

Thank God for Rob. I watched as he spun the journo round, pinned him in an arm lock, and told me to find some rope. There was a shed in the garden and I returned with a roll of binder twine. By now, the journalist was slumped in a chair, his eyes following our every movement. Rob had pulled the curtains on both windows and switched on a reading light. I gave him the binder twine and watched him tie the journo hand and foot.

"But what do you want?" he kept asking.

Rob just ignored him.

"This Irish story of yours," he said. "We need to know how far you've got."

The journo stared at him, then shook his head. No way was he going to help us out. Rob had a loose T-shirt over his jeans. From the front of his jeans he took out a small Army-issue hand-gun. The journalist stared at it. So did I.

Rob asked the question again. This time he got an answer.

"I took a call from a contact in Dublin ..." the journo began.

"When?"

"About five months ago."

"And?" Rob asked.

"Some villagers found a number of bodies washed up on a local beach. These people were naked. They'd been tied up hand and foot."

"How many bodies?" Rob asked.

"Four. There were post-mortems on all of them."

"And?"

"They all had the same injuries," said the journo. "Impact injuries plus severe frostbite. My contact said the impact injuries could have meant those bodies had fallen from a great height."

"Like out of a plane?"

"Yes."

"So what happened?" asked Rob.

"I went to Ireland."

"And?"

"I found out there'd been no inquest, no press coverage, no funerals, nothing. The bodies had just vanished. Along with the story."

"So what did that tell you?" Rob wanted to know.

"It told me ..." the journo was beginning to sweat "... that someone needed a big cover-up. They'd been applying a great deal of pressure."

"And where do you think that pressure came from?" Rob had the gun in the man's face.

"I've no idea."

"Think."

The journo stared at him. Rob once told me you can smell fear. He's right. He asked the question again, then put the muzzle of the handgun an inch above the journo's ear, pressing softly on the whiteness of his temple.

The journo swallowed hard, then closed his eyes.

"London," he whispered.

Chapter 9

Jerry's Story

We searched the cottage before we left. Upstairs, in a cupboard in the spare bedroom, we found a stash of files. We went through them one by one until we found the Irish story. The beach where the bodies had washed ashore was in County Kerry, near a village called Caherdaniel. The post-mortem had taken place in Kenmare. At the back of the file was a list of names and contact details. Three of the names were underlined and one of them had three stars beside it. The guy's name was Jerry Bull. He lived in North Wales. This, we both agreed, was our best chance of finding out some more.

Outside, it was raining. When I headed for the Porsche, Rob took me by the arm. The journo drove a beaten-up old Renault Clio. Rob must have lifted the keys when we were searching the house. The Generals would be watching for the Porsche. Better to swap cars.

I've known Rob for most of my life. We were best mates when we were kids and nothing had really changed. He'd once told me that he'd do anything to help if I ever got into serious shit, but what he was up to now was crazy. He had a career to think about, and kids. The journo would probably free himself within the hour. At which point, Rob and I had a big, big problem.

There had to be a reason Rob was doing all this. And there was.

"A few days ago I did the inspection in KidzStuff – the internment centre in Exeter," he said. "I asked for an up-to-date list of the internees. The guys in the front office put me in front of a PC and told me to help myself. I went through every name." He glanced across at me. "Then I found another list, just half a dozen names, priority targets they'd packed off north, some place they call the RC."

"What does that mean?" I asked.

"The Removals Centre," he said.

"And?"

"Anna was one of them."

****

We drove through what was left of the night, not saying very much. I think we both knew what risks we were taking, and why we were doing it. But that didn't make the prospect of the days to come any easier. Rob understood how enormous the task we'd set ourselves was. He's a commando, after all. But there's something in the mind-set he's got from working for the Marines that tells you that anything is possible if you want it badly enough. Like athletes, they believe in the power of focus.

It got light at four in the morning. By now we were in mid-Wales. To the north, we could just make out the blue mountains around Snowdonia. There was nothing on the roads and the few villages we passed seemed dead and empty.

An hour or so later, we stopped in a small country town for petrol. While Rob was filling the tank, I went across to the kiosk. I was in a bit of a daze by now, not thinking properly. I knew Jerry Bull lived in the Conway Valley but I hadn't a clue where that was.

The old man behind the counter was asleep. I sorted out a map and took it across. Then I saw the posters for the Olympics. There were three of them and on the biggest was a face I knew only too well. I was backing away, heading for the door, when the old man woke up. He eyed me a moment, then put out his hand to shake mine.

"My goodness, boyo." His eyes went to the poster. "What have you done to that pretty face of yours?"

****

We ran into the road-block an hour and a half later. Rob spotted it as we rounded a bend in a narrow valley. A couple of hundred metres away was a line of oil drums. Squatting on either side, half-hidden in the rocks beside the road, was a bunch of Bubs in full combat gear. Rob knew when a situation called for split-second decisions. He braked hard and pulled the car into a tight three-point turn. The first bullets shattered the windows behind me. Then came a louder bang as one of the tyres exploded. The car dipped to the left, then stopped.

I looked across at the driver's seat. Rob was slumped across the steering wheel, blood pumping from a hole in his throat. The firing had stopped now, and I reached across, to ease his body back against the seat, but it was hopeless. A second bullet had torn through his right eye. The spray of grey slime on the window behind him was brain tissue.

To be honest, I can't remember getting out of the car. All I could think of was Rob's face – shot to bits. I could hear shouting from the Bubs. They were standing up and two of them had set off down the road.

I took one look and began to run. I've never run faster in my life. I ran back round the corner, spotted a track up through the loose scree beside the road, and went for it. I pumped and pumped, forcing the cold mountain air deep into my lungs, and by the time I'd made the treeline there was still no sign of the Bubs. They must have stopped at the car, I thought. They must be seeing what I just saw. *My fault, bastard.*

I still had the map, thank God. I eased deeper into the trees, keeping an eye on the road below, and then set off at a fast jog, telling myself there was nothing I could have done to save Rob's life. The best thing now was to find Jerry Bull. His house was called Ty-Groes. I'd seen it on the map. A tiny road ran down to a small farm house beside a river. It was about 25 miles away. I was there by eleven o'clock.

There was a stand of trees on the hill above the house. I lay full length on the warm carpet of pine needles on the flank of the valley, scoping the farmhouse below. There was a Range Rover parked in front and a couple of horses in the paddock at the back. If you were looking for somewhere idyllic to hide yourself away, then this had to be it.

As I looked and checked my map again, I heard the distant growl of a diesel engine. Moments later, a black 4x4 pick-up swung in through the gate below. Two men got out.

Bubs. They knocked on the front door and went in. One of them came out minutes later, escorting a bulky figure in jeans and a blue shirt. They both got into the 4x4 and drove away. One Bub left, I thought. Plus whoever else might be inside the house.

My only option, I knew, was to wait. The sun edged steadily westwards and the shadows began to lengthen on the wooded slopes of the mountain beyond the river. Then, around five o'clock, a door opened and a woman stepped out with some dogs barking around her. Behind her was the Bub. He looked up towards the trees where I was still hiding, checked his watch, then went back inside. The woman whistled to the dogs and began to walk up the hill towards me.

It was the bigger of the two Labradors that found me first. I'd retreated deeper into the trees, nervous about what I was about to do. This woman, whoever she was, might well betray me. On the other hand, I had no choice but to trust my luck.

The dog, at least, seemed pleased to see me. It barked to begin with, then nuzzled my knee. I gave it a pat or two. I could feel the woman standing over me.

"Who on Earth are you?" she said. Posh voice. Puzzled.

I gave her my name. She knew who I was.

"You're the runner," she said. "You're the one who's making the stand. I read your thing on the internet. Very brave, if I may say so."

I thanked her. She was staring down at me.

"What on Earth happened to your face?"

I told her everything. Anna. Rob. The Bubs down the road. The lot.

"Terrible." She shook her head. "The times we live in, just awful."

This sounded hopeful.

"Is your husband's name Bull?"

"Yes," she said. "They've just taken him away."

"Why?" I asked.

"I wish I knew." She frowned. "I think I might have an idea, of course, but ..." she bent to slip a lead on the dog "... God knows."

She seemed to understand that I was on the run and I sensed she had a lot more to say, but she told me the Bub had given her fifteen minutes to walk the dogs and any minute now he'd come looking for her. At this, she turned to go back down the hill. Then she changed her mind and led the way to a thicket of trees out of sight from the farmhouse below.

"Jerry's in the RAF," she began. "Has been all his working life. The last couple of years he's been CO at an airbase up in Scotland. They've got spy jets, plus big transport aircraft. At first, before the take-over, he couldn't have been happier. It was his last posting before he retired. He loved it. The countryside, the people, everything."

She looked at me as if she expected me to say something. I asked her to carry on.

"Then the Generals took over and everything changed. Don't ask me what happened up there because Jerry's never told me but I just know it's something awful. He's changed. He's become a different man. I can see it. He comes home every two months for spells of leave. He can't sleep properly. He drinks too much. And when I ask what's going on, he just shakes his head."

"So what d'you think goes on up there?" I asked.

"I've no idea. And that just makes it worse. Then those horrible Bub people turned up this morning and just took him away. No explanation. Barely time to say goodbye."

"So what happens now? With your husband?" I said.

She looked at me for a long moment, then shrugged.

"I haven't a clue," she said. "All I know is that part of the base has been taken over by that big private security firm, the same lot that employ all the Bubs. Maybe that's got something to do with it. You tell me."

It was the dogs who heard the footsteps. They went tearing off down the hill, barking like mad. I began to follow them, then stopped. The Bub was 50 metres away. Mrs Bull had seen him too.

"Run," she said.

Chapter 10
The Removals Centre

The helicopters found me at dawn next morning. They'd been in the skies all night, criss-crossing the valley, using infra-red and searchlights. Infra-red can detect body heat. No matter how hard I ran, I had no chance.

A black 4x4 took me to Liverpool. I sat in the back between two Bubs. When I asked for something to drink, one of them gave me a bottle of water. We sped through the city until we got to the docks. They stretched north for miles, stacks and stacks of containers beside the huge cranes. At the far end, a high fence, topped with razor wire, went round a massive complex of sheds and warehouses. Once again, there were sandbags across the entrance and more Bubs asking for my ID.

I seemed to be back with the internees, except that this place was far more sinister. For once, my question sparked a reply.

"What's all this?" I'd asked.

One of the Bubs threw me a look. He was smiling.

"We call it the Removals Centre," he said. "You must have been a very bad boy."

****

The Removals Centre came as a shock. This was no trading estate superstore turned quickly into a prison for hundreds of internees. For one thing, there seemed to be far fewer inmates. For another, we were banged up in private cells. Someone had thought hard about this place, planned it properly, invested a bit of money. From the start I knew that getting out was probably impossible.

I learned more about this place from a printed, much-thumbed booklet that was in my cell. I would get three meals a day, served through the hatch in my cell door. There would be an exercise period of fifteen minutes every afternoon but any form of contact or talk with other prisoners was strictly forbidden. Before lock-up in the evening, I was allowed a five-minute visit to the showers at the end of my cell block. Otherwise I'd have to use the bucket beside my bed roll.

Days went by and I never got the promised exercise period. After pushing myself so hard for years on end, this began to mess with my head. I remembered the stand-up comic, Marcus, in Wall Fixings. He'd called the internment centre there 'limbo-land' and he was right.

The eerie silence outside my cell door was also getting on my nerves. Was anyone else in the place? I thought too hard about Anna, and about Rob. My best mate had died because I'd been stupid enough to buy a map. *My fault, bastard.*

When I got my meals, pushed through the hatch, I started to ask questions. What was going on? Why wasn't I allowed out for exercise? I was a world-class athlete, for God's sake. I *needed* to stretch my limbs. But no one answered. Only more silence, more frustration. And the first prickles of something else. Fear.

Then came the afternoon when a key scraped in the lock and I was led out into the blinding sunshine. My minder, it turned out, was only too happy to answer my list of questions.

"You want a spot of exercise? No problem, son. You want me to find you something to read? I'll do my best. Anything else, you just ask ..."

I nodded, still gazing round. The exercise yard looked like a playground. There was a high fence on all four sides. There were no other prisoners around – just me. I had fifteen minutes' exercise time so I set myself a target of 4000 metres.

I counted every one of them, sprinting alternate laps in the yard. In the hot sunshine, it felt good to be sweating again. At the end of the session, my minder threw me a towel. I'd seen a low brick-built shed nearby without windows. It seemed to go on forever and I wanted to know what it was. As promised, my minder was only too happy to answer my question.

"It's a meat safe," he said, "a huge deep freeze. All the beef from Argentina used to come in here for storage."

"And now?"

"Now?" He shot me his Scouse smile. "Now's different."

****

Just how different, I was soon to find out. It happened like this. The next day, in the morning, my minder was back again. He gave me a pair of Wellington boots, thick socks, a pair of sheepskin gloves, and a bulky winter anorak with a hood. Once I'd got dressed, he led me out again. We went round the exercise yard to a back entrance in the same meat safe building I'd noticed the day before. There was a roll-up metal door that covered the entrance. Just now the entrance was open, plenty wide and high enough for the white truck that had just backed in.

The minder walked me along the side of the lorry. Already I could feel the cold breath of the meat store beyond the back of the truck. A separate set of heavy doors to the safe itself yawned open and beyond was nothing but a thin grey mist as the freezing air condensed inside.

The minder told me to put up the hood on my anorak. The cold, he said, could be nippy on the ears. I nodded but I hadn't got a clue why I'd been brought here. I asked the guard and he pointed up at the rails which hung down from the ceiling. The rails connected to another set of rails in the back of the truck. The guard nudged me towards the meat safe.

"You'll find twenty or thirty inside," he said. "Just drag them out, one after the other, and push them into the truck, yeah?"

"Twenty or thirty what?" I asked. I was still staring up at the rails. When no answer came I looked round but the guard had gone.

I was already chilled to the bone but I stepped into the meat safe. The freezing mist made it impossible to get an idea of how big the place was. I couldn't see the walls and it felt huge, never-ending. I kept going, following the rails on the ceiling. Then, I began to make out shapes ahead. The closer I got, the more solid the shapes became. They were hanging by meat hooks from the rails. They were about my size. They were bound, hand and foot. They were upside down. And I saw they had faces.

I stopped, and looked back. There was nothing but the chill grey curtains of mist. I shut my eyes, tried to steady my pulse, tried to tell myself that this wasn't happening. It had to be a dream, a nightmare, some trippy drug they'd slipped me in my breakfast. Anything but the frozen naked corpses hanging by their ankles from the meat hooks in front of me, fingers and toes black with frostbite.

I opened my eyes again, took another couple of steps forward, cocked my head to get a better view. Then, as they must have planned, it hit me. It wasn't any old body. Not some stranger who'd overstepped the line and paid the price. But the one person in the world who could have brought me to this vile place.

Anna.

I reached out to touch her. Her flesh felt like cold marble. For a long moment I just stood there, staring at her. I felt ashamed to see her so naked, so icy, so dead. I should have done more. I should have come looking earlier, before she was ghosted away. I should have burst out of my sad little bubble, forgotten all about lap times and gold medals, tracked her down, protected her, kept her safe. Being Anna, she'd have made me join her cause, taught me how to protest, how to organise, how to hurt the Generals in thousands of little ways. In the end, they'd have caught us both. But that way, at least, we might have died together.

****

That night, and over the days to come, the feel of Anna beneath my finger-tips stayed with me. She didn't seem to have been hurt at all. I couldn't see any marks or bruises on her body. There might even have been a smile on her face. But the blueness of her eyes and that curl of the lips haunted me. Had the cold killed her? Had she hung there upside down and slowly frozen to death?

The more I thought about it, the longer the list of questions. Where did the truck take these corpses? And what happened at journey's end? Then I remembered what Mrs Bull had said about her husband's growing sense of torment. Was there a connection to the RAF base up in Scotland?

Maybe Jerry Bull had had to become part of this nightmare production line. Maybe these trucks were driven onto the big RAF transport aircraft and flown west, way out over the Atlantic Ocean. Dropped out of the back, the bodies would have the kinds of bruises the journo had heard about in western Ireland. Plus they'd be showing signs of frostbite.

I lay in my cell, staring up at the ceiling, trying to think what it must have been like. You'd hear the clunk as the pilot lowered the loading ramp at the back of the aircraft. Then would come the roar of the engines as he increased power and pulled the huge plane into a steep climb. The ramp at the back of the plane would already be open. I knew how easily the bodies in the truck moved on the overhead rails. One by one, stiff as boards, they'd drop from the truck, bounce towards the back of the plane, and then roll into thin air. No one would have touched them. Only gravity was to blame. And the next consignment was liable to include me.

Top athletes are winners. It won't happen to me, I told myself. Somehow I'd get through.

Chapter 11
Endgame

Or maybe not. It's the 18th of August, 2012. Apart from my minder, I haven't talked to another human being for weeks. Then, after an earlier lunch than normal, that same minder shows up.

He takes me outside and we end up in some kind of social club that must have been used by the staff. There's a bar at one end and a TV on the wall at the other. Half a dozen other prisoners are already seated in a semi-circle of chairs, staring up at the big plasma screen. I see the Olympic stadium, and the pattern of the hurdles on the running track. The stadium is full to bursting. It's the final of the 3000 metres steeplechase.

I know every one of these runners. I know their best times, what music they like, where they last went on holiday. I also know who'll probably win. I'm not there so it will be Abaka. He runs for Kenya.

The gun goes and they set off fast. Really fast. By the end of the third lap, the field has thinned and Abaka has tucked himself behind the pacemaker's shoulder. The pacemaker is an American, Drew Sheridan. Last time I saw him, we talked motorbikes.

Drew is pushing it on. By now, he should be knackered but somehow he seems to be running even faster. I look hard at his leg movement as he goes over the water jump but there's no sign of fatigue. At the start of the last lap, he begins to open a lead over Abaka.

If anything, it's the Kenyan who's beginning to tire. I can't believe what I'm watching.

The crowd are on their feet. In close-up, Abaka is reaching deep inside himself to summon that last surge of energy, that big handful of raw courage to close the gap and take Drew on the home straight.

It doesn't work. He's out of gas. And it's the American, arms raised, who crosses the line.

I look at the time. 7.57.63. It's an Olympic record but I've run faster. No question about it. I could have won gold.

The other prisoners are looking at each other. Like me, they've no idea what we're doing here, why we've been allowed to re-visit the outside world. On screen, Drew Sheridan is climbing onto the winner's plinth. He bends down for his medal. The Stars and Stripes flutter on the tallest flagpole. And then the band plays the American national anthem.

Oh, say! Can you see, by the dawn's early light,

What so proudly we hailed, at the twilight's last gleaming?

The music ends. The screen fades to black. There's a moment of total silence. Then a door opens on the other side of the room and three men walk in. They're wearing Wellington boots and thick winter anoraks. They have sheepskin gloves on. They look at us for a moment, then one of them nods towards the still-open door.

"Well, gentlemen?" he says softly. "Are you ready?"

Want More? Why not try these?

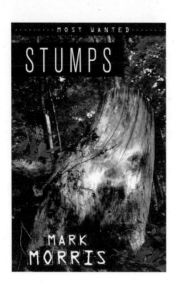

Stumps
by Mark Morris

Bridget and Colin have moved to the country for a fresh start. They hoped to leave their problems behind. But the darkness has followed them. At night, Bridget sees things. Colin's losing his grip. And the weird stumps in the garden seem to have a strange power over them. Their dream life is slowly turning into a nightmare. And one secret will not remain buried ...

Sawbones
by Stuart MacBride

They call him Sawbones: a serial killer touring America kidnapping young women. The latest victim is Laura Jones — the daughter of one of New York's biggest gangsters. Laura's dad wants revenge — and he knows just the guys to get it. Sawbones has picked on the wrong family ...

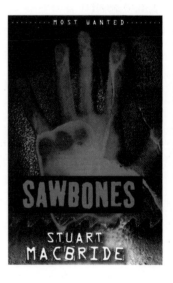

You can order these books directly from our website at
www.barringtonstoke.co.uk